AF425290

Nykkynn's

THIS IS FER

BAMBI

ISBN 979-8-9873039-0-0
Self-Assembled then Published and Printed
by Kindle Direct Publishing

Shout out ta muh famleh. Gotta love em'.

Bobby Dollar's Claim:

HOW IT STARTED

The reason I was drivin' drunk was because the Deer made me do it- he even had a gun pointed at me, threatened to kill me. I know it sounds crazy but you need to read the whole dang thing. I'll start from the beginnin' –I wanna be extra clear, don't mind my country twang. It was a sunny day outside when it all began, the trees were chirpin', blue skies and honey bees, it was the perfect day for killin'. I had my guns ready, we packed em' up in the Jeep and everything. I got my gear on, the whole camo get up, the spare sniper scopes, I got it all. I was born to kill for sport. It wouldn't be fun to kill for any less. My boy, Brock Dollar –you can just look at him, he was built to be a Juggernaut. He still struggles in basic division, but he's got a mean flex. My boy's seen everythin', we've gone killin' down in the deeper part of the woods. I got my 45. We got them quads out in them woods, rippin' roads into the grass, we're all over the dang place with those things. I got my rifles strapped to the back, we might as well be Golfers. Put a hole in one deer.

We gone up to the tops of mountains, killin' in the ravines, the woods, the Cougar trail- I had to kill me one of those just because she was gonna attack me. These back-woods bitches can't survive without diggin' their teeth into your life. You gotta kill em' quick. Pew pew. Do it now before she's got ya. She's a hungry Gato. I carried mine around my shoulders like a fur scarf. I gotta pretty one. Anyway, we seen it all.

So like I said, we had all our gear, ready, it's in the back-a-my Red 4x4 Jeep truck, lifted suspension, designed to ride over the balls of the Earth without a single tumble; and we took off from the Cabin. It's 4 AM, we're goin' like 40 up the windy roads to go meet up with Michael Taylor, the Slaughterhouse owner in the Town. Michael Taylor cut your bodies up real nice, make it presentable. It's a dang art, is what it is. I'm an eater myself, I see him coppin' up all those body parts, my mouth just waters like 120 degree sweat. I gotta put my dang sunglasses on just to look at it.

We all got our Flannels on underneath the camo; Red collar means 'Team Bloodthirsty'. If I see y'all off in the distance with a Blue Collar, might shoot ya.

So we meet up with muh friend, Michael. He gets in the Jeep with his 2 boys, Tommy and Doug Taylor. We're all in the Jeep. We go up the mountain, we get there, and the skies are blue, it's lookin' great. We look down the mountain. We're lookin' for some serious game, I'm itchin' for a trigger puller. Brocks got his gun down like a military master, he takes it apart, puts it back together with a Timer and everythin'. I suddenly see this Deer. Not the one that was in the Convertible City car you pulled us over in, this was a different one, she was a female. She was a fine piece of ass, I saw that in the distance, I even told Michael, "That ass is mine." I told him flat out, because I already knew, I saw the future, I told him, "Michael Taylor, … I 'm gonna say it for the record, because I want it all on the record. I'm tellin' you right now, …that Ass is mine."

Michael knew we'd **both** be eatin' *that* one. Both of us, the whole family. I got my rifle ready. We were up on the side of the road on the mountain, closer to the bottom of the mountain, and I just saw that deer standin' there. I got my rifle ready, put my scope on it, screwed it in and everythin', pointed up at the deer and in 1 shot- POW!

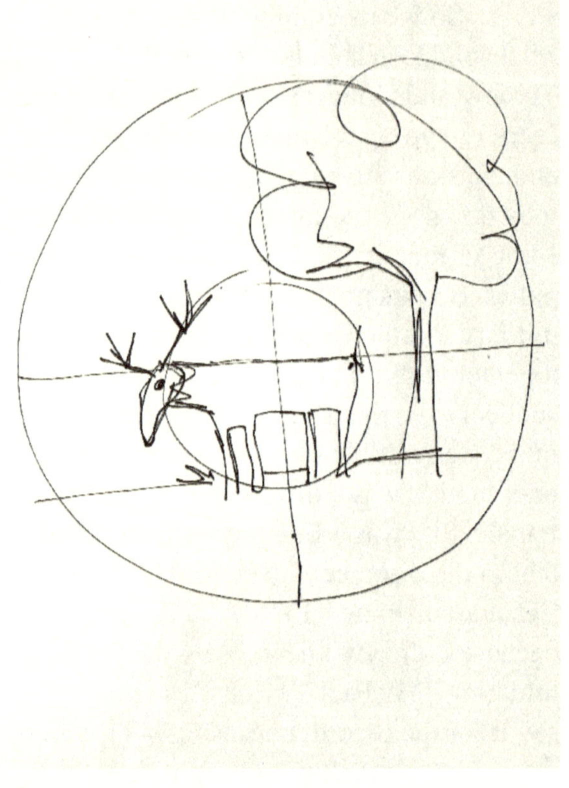

Look it this, I even drew pictures. This is
what I saw when I was lookin' through the
scope. This is a picture of the last moment of
the Deer's life before I shot the Hell out of
it. See how I put the line above the Deer's
back? I always do that before firing, just to
make sure my shot is steady, make sure I kill
that son-um-itch in one hit. No bullet
wasted.

…Anyway, Shot's fired, I mean it was loud. She was struck down by my gaze. I looked right at her and she knew she was mine. I pulled that trigger, and nailed her right in the heart. She was dead in seconds.

Now, you might be asking, "Okay well, where is that deer then? Why do you have a deer with Antlers in a Convertible?" I understand the confusion, and believe me, what I'm about to tell you sounds just as crazy to me as it does to you, but this happened that day, just hear me out now.

We were all happy, okay? People were yellin' n' shoutin', We got down the hill side to the deer laying on the ground, Michael's got his cellphone out takin' pictures and postin' them online. The boys Tommy and Doug are posing with the dead Deer there, I think Tommy did a B-boy pose. You can see the picture on Michael's profile, they're really good, Michael's sons are talented individuals. Doug is actually a Deer Whisperer, he just knows how to talk to em', and he understands em' in a way that's a magic psychic ability. It's on that Nostradamus level. So, like I said, I picked that deer up and it dragged behind me up the hill for about 50 yards or so, I got that heavy carcass up the hill.

Well, that whole time, while we were down there, I didn't know this but, there was another Deer watchin' in the bushes. No one noticed it but I did, I just got that hunters eye, I'm always lookin' for somethin' to kill, and I saw him. He was in there. He was lookin' at me with those crazy eyes. The kinds of eyes of violence. It was risin' up in him, I could see it. I seen it happen to somebody when they snort their first line on the toilet seat of a bar bathroom in Barstow California. The Deer was angry. He was ready to do somethin' bout it. Goes up the hill outta the bush, I know it's him, everyone sees him, and he comes chargin' at us up the hill, I drop the Deer to grab my gun, I got that 45 on my leg. I grab the gun, the dead deer I shot earlier, drops n' hits the ground. I go to shoot- the safety's on because I'm such a careful user of the firearm.

It's too late, the Deer attacks Tommy- his antlers impale Tommy's back, there's blood all over the side of the mountain, Tommy's stuck to his antlers- I'm firin' the gun off, I can't hit a dang thing because he's buckin' around everywhere like a rodeo n; I don't wanna blow Tommy's dang head off. Michael goes to get his gun, the Deer uses his antler tip to chuck the gun away from Michael, and Tommy's screaming bloody murder.

Doug starts usin' his psychic Deer powers to telepathically communicate with the Deer. The Deer stood on its hind legs, took away Michael's gun and pointed it at us while it was screechin' "Mhhheeeerreeerr!". Doug started to interpret the Deers psychic message, "He says, Put the gun down."

I said No, I didn't trust that Deer a dang minute. Then the Deer started yelling out real loud, "Mheeeerrrreeeeeerrrrrrr!!!!" It *scared* me. He really *meant* it, you could feel it rumble in your soul. I said, "Let me take the Deer, and we'll go our separate ways. No need to shoot anybody." He yelled again, "Mheeeerrrrrrererrrrr!" and Doug said, "You're all going to die!" But I pulled the trigger, the bullet ricocheted off the barrel of the Deer's gun as the Deer fired *his* gun, and we both missed. The Deer's guns outta bullets now, he has enough trouble pullin' the trigger with his dang hooves, I ran up to the Jeep with Brock. Michael yells, "Bobby Dollar, My son! My Son Tommy is stuck to his antlers!"

That boy was dead, he aint breathin'. Michael can't believe it, he's still livin' in a fantasy back there.

I get up to the top with the dead Deer carcass, the other one charges at me, he tries to attack my boy but you know Brock. He just grabbed that Deer by the Antlers jiggled his head 'round while pullin' Tommy's dead body off it. Tommy's a falling rag doll. The Deer grabs his gun away, and that's when we got in the Jeep and started drivin' off basically, I threw Tommy onto the roof of the Jeep n' used my Elastic Net Strap to hold em' down, then I threw Deer on top of em, and strapped that down on top of em'. We all got in the Jeep, the Deers firin' that rifle off all crazy like, bullets everywhere, Michael got shot in the back of his left arm. We get in, we drive off. That was it, that was the last we thought we were gonna see of that Deer.

I never seen a Deer fire a gun until today when that one did it. He was a different breed-a-deer, ain't never seen it before. He stood up on his hind legs like a man and started runnin' after us, takin' our guns n' all that. It was crazy. Michael took pictures, it's on his social media page. We took Tommy to the Hospital, they got him on life support. I told Brock, "I don't think that Deer was normal." And Brock looked at me and I'll never forget what he said to me, straight in my eyes, he said, "It was a Violent Venison of Vengeance." And he was right. I never dun seen no amount-a-chaos in my life. But it doesn't stop there. No!

We drove back up the mountain back to Michael's Cabin, and the Deer was waitin' there for us! He was there! The dang Deer was there! …With a stick! So, the Deer ran up n' started beatin' the Jeep with the stick, that's why it got all scratched up! You'd think it would be from the tree branches in nature when we're 4-byin' but, I can dance that Jeep up a rock cliff like a ballerina. Not a scratch on it, then this Deer comes along and scratches the hell outta the sides, the doors, they all got indentations. Like- actual indentations, I want it on the record so my Insurance knows it really happened. It's *legal.* Don't really matter though, eventually I got that Jeep replaced, but don't let me get ahead-a-myself.

Anyway, we got away. I drove as fast as I could away from that Deer because it was on a mission. It was after me. I was there. We were weavin' the windin' roads and this Deer was chasin' after us, keepin' up cuz you gotta go slower around turns n' everythin', but I finally outran him. Told the boys, we gotta go to the City side n' hide out in a Grocery store for awhile until this blows over. My boy Brock was so stressed out, he started getting anxious so, when we got to the Grocery store, I bought him a 30 pack to help him relaxed.

But that's the thing, I thought we got away right? *Wrooong*. Somehow he hitched a ride on the back of a flatbed tow truck and saw the jeep! He was there, in the parking lot, he knew where we were! He knew we was in the Grocery store hidin' from him.

He broke into my Jeep and stole one of my huntin' rifles and started loadin' it full of Ammunition in the parking lot while we was in the Grocery store, he was schemin' hard. We were in line at the store. It was me, Michael, Brock and Doug in the store. We get up to that part of the line where the conveyer table thingy is and Brock put the case-a-30 on there and I looked out the window with huntin' eyes n' I said, "Shit-titties, it's that dang Deer again!" He was out there with the gun, 50 yards off in the distance of the lot, pointin' it right at us! I yell "Duck!" We all get down- the Cashier looks around fer-a real-life Duck- shot's fired hit the cashier like a car crash, poor woman wasn't even worth eatin'!

We ran off with the beer, I left $40 bucks on the counter even though the wind from the gunshot might've blown it away! It was twirlin' around like a Forest Gump feather when we took off. We're gone!

The Deer comes into the Grocery store with a loaded rifle, and he's aimin' at me from the other end of the store- we was runnin' towards the back, we wanted a cinder block wall between us until we could escape back to the Jeep. We were in the pharmacy, and the Doctors back there were screamin' n' everythin'. We ran into the storage and POW! That dang shot went right through the swing doors and messed up an entire pallet of orange juice n' stuff.

We ran out the back door, it's that metal kind. But the Police were there, and they thought we was stealin' the Beer! So, we ran back inside, but the Deer was there, and came out, and the Police all had their guns pointed at us, and the Deer had the rifle pointed at them, and he was yellin', "Mheerrrreerrerrreeerr!!!" It was all raspy in such. Sent a chill down everyone's spine. I was ready to dump a shit right there, I could have, I would have, I should have, but I'm a tight ass. I remember lookin' into the eyes of that Deer again, and I seen that same crazy eyed expression. He wanted to kill those police officers, he wanted the real thing.

Doug interpreted the Deer's thoughts with his telepathic Psychic abilities, "He says to mind your own business or we're all gonna die!" I looked over at Michael, and he knew we were in deep,… real deep…, soggy deep. The Deer made us go back into the Grocery store slowly. The Red and Blue lights were flashin' all over the store soon, the place was surrounded. I didn't know what the hell was gonna happen next, I couldn't tell if I was gonna be dead soon or in handcuff soon- I didn't know. All I knew is this Psycho Deer was pissed off and he was gonna kill me. He was gonna kill me good. He was gonna punch a bullet hole right through my skull like any Psycho Deer would, right there in the back of the Grocery store. He was ready, he was gonna do it, but the place was surrounded. He knew he needed leverage, he needed it real bad.

I told the Deer, "You're outta your dang mind if you're gonna get outta here with his dead. You can't get out alive now. They're all gonna hunt ya down n' kill ya!" and the deer yelled back at me "Mheeerrrreeeerr!!!" and Doug said, "Ya'lls gonna die with me!" and I told the Deer,

"You sick piece of shit! You're gonna git
yourself killed just to kill me! You only got
one way out! You gotta hold us hostage!"
and the Deer yelled "Mheerreerreerr!!!" but
louder this time. Doug was horrified, "He
says we're gonna walk out the front door!"

I yelled back at him, "You're gonna
die!"

So, finally we got to the front of the
store where the cash registers were and their
lights were flashin' everywhere, and the
Police on the Bull horn started sayin'
somethin'. I think it was a negotiator, and he
said, "No one needs to get hurt," and "We
have the place surrounded," and "We'd like
to cut a deal."

The Deer made his demands through
Doug, had Doug yellin' out the door, "He
want's a clear path to the Jeep! He says he's
rigged the whole parking lot with
explosives! He could push a button with his
hoof at any moment and you'll all die!" and
the Negotiator outside said, "Alright! Let
him through! Let him through!"

So, he made us walk out the door
first with his rifle to our backs, out in front
of everyone. The sun's out, there's people
watchin' from across the street, I'm
schemin' on a way to stop the Deer, Brocks

carryin' the 30-pack, Michael gets to the Jeep first. We was all in a wall formation around the Psycho Deer, and the Deer was last, standin' on his hind legs with that rifle out. The 4 of us go to the Jeep when the Negotiator yells, "He's bluffing! Open fire!" I jump in the jeep, we're all in there, the Deer's still outside the Jeep when the shots go off and start hitting the jeep!

Turns out the Deer is a marksman, he started pickin' the officers off one by one, using the Jeep as a shield, the barrel of the gun over the hood! Pow! Pow! Pow! Pow! Just, over n' over, the Deer was a complete psychopath! I never seen anything like it in my life. I start the Jeep, lock the doors, slam on the gas, and knock the Deer back! He drops the Rifle as we're gettin' away and I thought we finally got away. I thought, okay, that's it. The police got him now! They're gonna kill that son-um-itch! But no… the Deer lived. He mowed em' all down, half of them ran away, the Deer was too good. He got that 'Deer Eye', it's gotta rectangle or somethin'.

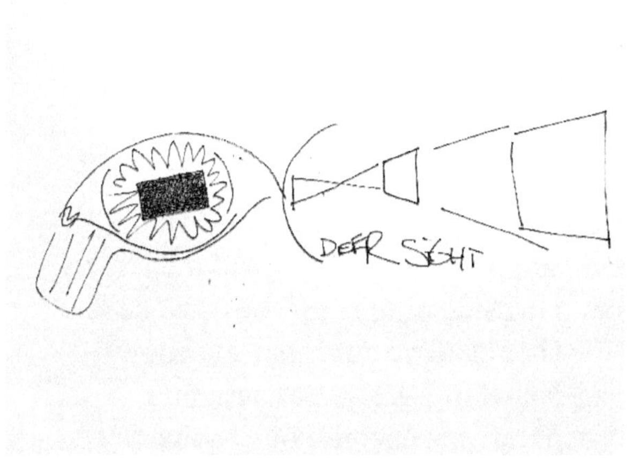

This is what a Deer's eye looks like. So obviously Deers can see differently than regular people cause people gots the round eye. Deers got that Latterbox widescreen eye to avoid gettin' hunted down by wild predators. They need to be able to look the Hell around real good. It's like Deers live their whole lives in a Movie theater, but this Psycho Deer was playin' Video games.

We thought the Psycho Deer was stuck in the city side now, we were headed back to the mountain town to go home, finally get some kinda sanctuary from the Deer, but it only got worse… We're on the highway back up the mountain, the Deer is riding a Harley Davidson. He rides the bike right up beside the Jeep and jumps from the bike onto the hood-a-the Jeep- his legs slidin' into the windshield, his hooves breakin' through. The Jeep swervin' all over the road, into oncoming traffic, and then slams into the side of the mountain to a dead stop! We should all be dead, but somehow we lived, somehow, we all got out of the Jeep. The Deer was unconscious on the ground, still breathin' but knocked the Hell out. The Jeep was totaled, there ain't no way to get it runnin'. We had to find a way to shoot the Deer before the Deer woke up.

We fought over the gun! It fired off and popped a Diesel truck tire and caused it to swerve out of control until tipping on it's side and completely blocking the entire highway. Cars runnin' into it, they all explode. Fireworks up into the sky, it was bad- real bad. I started fightin' the Deer, fist against Hoof. It got real serious real quick in the middle of the road.

He underestimated my brawlin' abilities. I got that swing on me, I'll hammer a Lego into a tree, hit em' in the Pelosi. I punched that dang Deer's lights out a few times, but he kept gettin' back up. My knuckles started to hurt but I punched him in the face again and then he punched me hard with his hoof and I wanted to cry. I was gonna cry right there, I felt like it. I whimpered a little, but then I got it back together, knocked that dumb Deer out good this time. I looked at the Deer and thought, "I needa Mortal Kombat Fatality right now," and before you know it, my fist was smackin' that Deer's face clean off. It felt real, like magic in muh arms. He started screamin, "Mheeeeeeeeeeeerrrr!!!" and I was so scared right then n' there, that shrill just shivers ya dang timbers.

Brock suddenly came out grabbin' the Deer by the Antlers and forcin' him into a lane where the Deer then got hit by a car in the pile up. It gave us a chance to run away, er-else that dang Deer would still be tryin' to kill us! And I couldn't shoot the dang thing because my bullets were scattered all over the highway- I was so pissed off- y'all know how expensive that shit is? I didn't wanna pick em' up n' risk throwin' out muh back.

I told my boy and the Taylors, "We gotta go by the Ammo store before we go home er' we ain't gonna have a chance against this son-um-itch, I tell ya what." So we waited fer the Tow truck to show up to my Jeep from a far distance, to see if the Deer would wonder off into the forest n' everythin'. Michael was so pissed about Tommy still, he was ready to kill that Deer. He lit up a Cigar and puffed it until the Police showed up. I thought he quit smokin' a long time ago, but he had some kind of revelation about himself in the midst of all the activity, and started lookin' traumatized and vengeful-like. He started starin' off into space like a star gazer watching a dumb ass comet. He's been lyin' to me the whole time, he secretly smokes Tobacco on Saturdays. At least, that's how much he *used* to smoke, because from here on out, I just seen him… runnin' round… with that **dang** cigar in his mouth. Doug's forehead got shiny… like a bubble. His Psychic abilities made his forehead shiny. And, Brock… I seen him stare at a grain of sand for 5 minutes… That's my boy, nothin' fazes him. That's pure concentration waitin' to squeeze the Hell out of a trigger. -Pop a Deer from up to a hundred yards.

All the People started gettin' out of their crashed vehicles on the road, piled up with a line of stopped cars at the crash. There was Kyle the Truck driver. The whole thing was on its side, taking up 3 of the 6 lanes. Then there was Kathy in her little white car, looked like a cupcake squished between two books on a shelf- you know what I'm talkin' bout. And there was Jordan the Tech geek in his sporty Kia. They all started talkin' to each other n' everythin'. So Kyle the Truck guy walks up to the Deer, we're watchin' this from the distance, Kyle walks up, and starts talkin' to everyone about the Deer, thinkin' someone hit the Deer, and it caused this Pile up. I told Michael, that Deer's gonna wake up…

Michael spit on the ground and said maybe Kyle has a gun. So this crowd of people from the car accident are lookin' down at the deer and all 4 of us walk up to em' from the distance shoutin' "Shoot it!"

"Shoot the Deer!"

Everyone was standin' around shocked for the moment and this Karen bitch came out, she's real mean, come walkin' up and she started blamin' us for the car accident and all that nonsense. I told that bitch to get a pull up bar. She got mad.

We're all tellin' them to shoot the Deer, Karen's speakin' Japanese, Everyone just standin' around in shock. Michael finally walks up to the Truck driver and he says to the guy, "You gotta gun?"

And he got all defensive, started gettin' heroic n' everythin' and I straight up told everyone to shut their dang mouth n' let me speak here. I told em' this Deer is psychotic and it needs to get put down- put more lights out than a Christmas Street. I says to Kyle, don't be a pussy- n' go get yer gun, and shoot this dang Deer in the face multiple times. But Kyle had different opinions. First of all, he was Transgender. I don't know what that's like, I'm not Vegan, but I'm sure of one thing, it's not common fer gay people to own a gun. Brock already knew, he was offended, he says to the guy, "Transgenders don't have guns."

But then Kyle got offended and started yellin' at us, and I told him to shut-up. I told him to go get his gun n' shoot this Deer, and then later, when he starts to have feelin's again, we can talk about it. Brock got stupid though, he says to the guy, "I don't even think you know how to hold that gun." But it was a good thang, 'cause Kyle challenged us to look at the guns in his tipped over diesel truck. But it was too late because the Tow trucks and the Police arrived, n' all the sudden, the Deer woke up.

The four of us were between crashed cars followin' Kyle to the truck when it all happened. The Deer got up, people started backin' away from it, n' the four of us got down because we knew what was about to happen. The Deer started goin' on a rampage, impalin' people with his antlers and swinging em' around in the air like screamin' pizza doe. I looked over at Kyle and says "y'all better run to that truck, Hermafo. You better go get them guns quickly." But the Deer was runnin' for him. He was on top of the crashed cars, hoppin' from hood to hood!

Kyle got into his Semi through the bottom broken windshield. Kyle grabbed his shot guns from behind the seat as they were strapped up to the inside of the Semi, cause that's what he told me where they were. I guess he got to them as the Deer came up and started rammin' his antlers into the windshield but Kyle got out, and aimed to shoot down at the Deer, but the deer rammed the windshield as he fired. He misfired, fell off the Semi, n' broke his neck. The 4 of us, we was already runnin' back to the police officers that showed up, and right when we got to em' the cops seen it behind us, they was pointin'. I didn't even know it until that first officer pointed it out. He said that Deer right there's gotta gun, and I already knew. I ran faster. There was gunfire everywhere, we got behind the police car 'cause there was ricochet bullets ever-where. The Deer had run all the way up to the Police cars while shootin' n' started attackin' police! I would've shot the dang thing with a Shotgun if the Police didn't officiate themselves, and then do a horrible job by dyin'. So we ran for our lives, we were far away from that scene, and I don't know what happened after that, I was just runnin'.

I think I saw some trees… maybe I crossed a street somewhere… Anyway I said, forget the Jeep, I'll report it stolen. Just kiddin', I already got a new one.

So the Taylors ended up sleepin' at the Cabin, and my Wife, Betty Dollar had made us dinner. I was starvin'. We had Deer Tri-tip with mashed potatoes and butter… salt n' pepper, then went to sleep. Well… I couldn't sleep deep enough… I had my eyes shut but my mind was alert like a bat's ears. My sonar was a hummin' a deep penetration

into the surroundin's, n' I could sense
something out in the woods. I could hear it
in the dead-a-night, it was a hauntin' rustle.
It was a wild animal out there… tryin' sneak
a bullet through the window… It's just not
fair… I don't hunt down somethin' that ain't
awake, I'd expect no different across the
predatory spectrum.

I got my revolver out from the
dresser drawer next to a box of bullets and
also another revolver because 2 revolvers is
better than 1 revolver. It's just common
sense. I got them out, and loaded them, and
started crawlin' round the Cabin, looking
out the windas… lookin' *oooout* there… I
seen the bushes movin' in the moon light. I
knew he was out there. He'd been plottin'.

He'd been out there in the night with
a flashlight and a map writin' down every
step he's gonna take to get into the Cabin n'
shoot me, but I Knew better. I got my
residential camouflage on. I dressed up like
a stack of large cardboard boxes and started
movin' around the house. Ya see, I cut these
hoola hoop sized holes in the top and bottom
of the boxes and then walked aroun' the
cabin pushin' the boxes with me and
pointin' my guns ahead, ready to fire at any
second.

I went to the kitchen and opened the refrigerator carefully. I made sure that when I got there, that my hands weren't exposed, which means, the box has to make contact with the refrigerator door handle and allow just enough space for the handle to be grabbed without showing the hand itself, grabbin' the refrigerator door handle. That means the box has to be tipped towards the window to help hide my hand from bein' seen. If my hand does show, it could blow my cover and alert that Deer that I'm in the boxes. Now I know this seems slightly paranoid but, …I've been huntin' my whole dang life, I know what I'm doin'. There's a Deer with a gun out there… and he's not buckin' round.

When I got to the Refrigerator door, in the silence, I was detectin' a motion out there. In the distance beyond the trees of the Cabin, I heard a gun click…, like a scope is bein' gently placed into position of the rifle barrel. I knew it was him. I felt him schemein' balls deep in the bushes of the darkness. He was waitin' for me to show myself, but he hadn't seen me yet. All he could see was a stack of boxes in the kitchen, checkin' the refrigerator fer a bag of Italian Dry Salami. It was too suspicious. I slowly ducked down inside the boxes and suddenly the top box where my head and upper shoulder were, just exploded by a 44 Smith & Wesson Special bullet- shattered muh dang window and put a hole in the wall. I hadn't even got my hands on the Salami yet. That's when everyone in the house woke up n' gun shots started chopping up the house. The Taylors roll off the couches n' gab their guns from under the couch, blastin' out the sliding glass winda to the porch. It's completely decimatit. The whole inside of the Cabin's been hit by bullets, I don't even know how many Deers gotta be out in the woods to be shootin' at us like this, it's a dang Deer Contra. I get the Salami. I'm lookin' out the boxes into the darkness while the Taylors are shootin' out there. Then Brock walks in with a machine gun and start mowin' down the bushes outside like it's landscapin', ain't never seen nothin' like it before. After he stopped firin' the barrels smoked up, got that bullet smell in the house and it smelt good. I heard Michael get up with that Cigar in his mouth, just lightin' up. He says he don't see nothin', so he steps out onto the porch and Doug yells, "Dad, Be careful," but I knew he was bein' stupid. He was bein' a dang fool, I'd never step out there without a light, but that mess got him puckered up. He was out there smokin' that cigar, looking round in the bushes. You'd think he lost his truck keys.

I even told Michael, ya'll better get yer ass back in the Cabin now, ya hear? No more messin' round now, there's a son-um-itch out there not givin' a dang now, ya'll just better get in the Cabin. Dang Deers gonna blow yer dang brains out if ya don't get back in the Cabin. But he didn't listen…

He saw a rabbit in the Bush. And he said, oh it's just a dang rabbit, but then I looked, and I saw stick comin' out of the bush. It was a bamboo stick with a fishin' line on it. And the Fishin' line was connected to the Rabbit's head and Tail.

I yelled out, That ain't no Real Rabbit, that's a Rabbit on a Stick! And that's when Michael looked up and notices the Antlers in the bush in the moon lit sky! He was looking at him from behind the bush leaves, he was peerin' through there, right at him! Michael screamed like he knew it was too late, but I fired my Colt 45 and it snapped the tip of his antlers, bumpin' his shot, and the Deer's rifle bullet grazes Michael arm real bad! Blood squirtin' out everywhere like a katsup packet.

This is exactly what it looked like when the
Psycho Deer tried to lure Michael out to the
bushes with that dead rabbit on a stick. It
looked just like this.

I bust out of my boxes n' start firin' my 45 at the Deer, Pow! Pow! Pow! I mean I went Pow! Like real loud! It sent shockwaves through the Cabin. I dang near created Time travel with these gun shots, the room was just Wam! Wam! Wam with these shockwaves. It was dang near music. I should've gotten a *Cellphone* snap.

The Deer somehow, doesn't get shot, but it looks like his gun is empty, so he drops the rabbit-on-a-stick and runs off into the darkness. Everybody was standin' there stressin' out but it ain't over yet. I got me a mean ass Rottweiler chained up in the basement named 'Boomer'. She's a little girl that can smell the stench of a liar from up ta 50 miles away. She gotta nose on er' that'll smell your daughter's lost virginity. I went down there real fast, and she was real hungry, real mean. I had to put the suit on. I got that leash and walked up the stairs with her bitin' the shit out muh arm to the top, and she sniffed the dead rabbit out in the bushes once I got er' up there, started pullin' the leash, leadin' us out into the woods with our heat packed in clips. Brock got out the Assault Rifle.

The dog dragged us out further into the darkness, we all got flashlights. There's a flashlight on Brock's AK. Doug's even gotta flashlight on his forehead to do electrical. We get out there real deep, we're past the G spot, we're hittin' the wall. Brocks got his gun ready, he's so anxious to pull the dang trigger, I tell ya, that's muh boy. We found a shack. Looks like an old haunted house built in the woods by an Autistic Boy Scout. The Dog was takin' us right into there, got our flashlight runnin' along the outside surface of the dilapidatit structure. The winds blowin' on the house, it's gotta howl to it. Boomer's barkin' like crazy, he knows somethin' in there. We walk in the house, and it's full of photographs on the wall of each of us. Like some sick buck is plottin' against us. There's a bunch of marker lines all over the walls and different kindsa stolen guns n' everything. Like we found the hide out. Like we found the layer of the Psycho Deer out in some abandoned haunted ass house. He must've lost it a long time ago. Like he seen us shoot Deers before. Guilty as charged. I shot all kindsa Deer, blow a hole right through a Deer so a crane can pick it up off the side of the mountain with a hook. I'm sick as Hell when I'm hungry. Better believe a dang *it*.

The Dots er stars, n' then that's the moon.
Then there's trees behind the house. I put
smoke in the chimney as wavy lines so it
gives it that outdoors hospitality feelin'.
Then there's Boomer pullin' that leash,
sniffin' a line all the way to the bottom of
the rabbit hole.

Doug started to lose it. We had to calm him down but he couldn't take it. I says we head back to the Cabin, the Deer's nowhere to be found. Brock had to drop 20 so he went out behind a bush. Soon as he was done, we went back down the hill with Boomer and when we got back to the Cabin, somethin' wasn't right. I could feel it, it was deep inside muh tummeh, I needed some grub.

We walked up to the house, to the back sliding glass door, and we see the Deer in there, with my wife, Betty Dollar, dead-asleep bein' carried by the Deer- she sleeps real heavy, make an Insomniac jealous just like Narcoleptics do. He walked on his hind legs with Betty over his shoulder and started runnin' out the front door to evade our walin' gun shots! I run into the Cabin over to the front door, he's throwin' Betty's ass in the back, passed out all over the seat of the Convertible, n' he's jumpin' in the front seat. The gun shots sparkle the car side as it backs out of the driveway with an aggressive jolt- got Betty's legs up in the air flappin' in the wind while the Deer screamin' "Mhheeeerrrreeeeerrr!" I's so pissed off, he was just takin' off with my wife into the night. I was *so* mad now. I's mad before, but now he bucked with the wrong Man. Imma find his ass. Imma put that ass down is what I's gonna do. I's gonna find him. I's gonna make sure that buck was buckin' fer the last time. But it got complicatit. He took off in a convertible. We had to pack into Betty's little Nissan Pick up truck, Boomer, Brock n' Doug were in the back on the truck bed.

We went racin' out into the night after that Convertible. Brock was aimin' his rifle over the roof of the truck at the Deer, firing bullets at the Deer. He blew holes in the windshield. The Deer kept swervin' though n' Brock's not designed for that, he's a Sniper shot, he needs a calm environment, a space to breathe, knock the apple off a new born baby at 100 yards. Put em' on top of a movin' truck, couldn't hit'is own face. But he punctures that convertible up real good. It went from Malibu to Swiss in a matter of a couple minutes. That upholstery's gonna raise the insurance. The dash alone is smokin'. I told Michael, we needa push this son-um-itch off the road real good if we's gonna stop em'. Smacked that Dang convertible on the side and it went veerin' off to the right down a dirt road further into the woods.

I slammed on the brakes and put it in reverse. The Convertible was already pretty far down the trail. I Slammed on the gas n' we was rollin' through. It was a race now, he's windin' through the woods- dead-a-night. Were right behind em'. His ass is mine. I got up real close to the back of his car, and the dirt road lead to a main road that lingers back into the city. He turned out to the city n' I followed right behind em'. Got up right real close, and Brock jumped from the truck over to the Convertible n' they started fightin' on the straightaway. It was like some Karate stuff. Brock got in the back seat, the Deer swung his antlers around and Brock just grabbed em' n' the Deer would have to yank em' away. Then the Deer started swingin' his hoof at Brock but Brock evades too good, he's a natural born winner. Brock slaps the Deer on the nose n' that pissed em' right off right there, son-um-itch got out his dang seat and threw another punch at Brock, n' they both start throwin' punches. The Deer standing on the seat as the car veers outta control, it was suicidal. Doug knew it, he jumped right in there, got in the front seat while the Deer and Brock are stepping all over the car, hittin' each other in the face.

We get into a neighborhood on the outskirts of the city, n' the road wer it goes right into a T at the highway. Ya gotta pick right er' left. Brock knocks the Deer off the car! The Deer runs off, slams into a fence- put a dang hole in a fence that goes into someone's back yard. We get to the T in the road, the house with the backyard is on the right corner. We pulled up in that bitch real quick. Saddle up. That Deer went right through that fence, dove into it. It went right back in there, shattered the back- sliding glass door into the kitchen, the people inside are screamin' outta there minds, Deer goes into the guys bed room and pulls the Man of the house's midnight pistol out of the night stand. We knew what he was doin, we ain't stupid. I didn't even knock, we rolled up in that there house like we owned the place, but the Deer came out blastin', Pow! Pow! I ran out the front door, past the convertible, across the street, hopped a dang fence into the house backyard.

Michael Taylor got in a Shoot out in the house. Brocks around the corner takin' cover and Doug's sneakin' round back-the-house, we gotta put this son-um-itch down. He's blastin' Pow! Pow! The kids are screamin', the whole neighborhood's lights are turnin' on, people are walkin' outta their house like a dang siren is goin' off. High Class neighborhood turned Ghetto in 5 minutes, It ain't even my fault, I just happen to be there.

Michael got shot again in the leg, the dumbass, n' Brock had to go in there n' pull his ass out while Boomer's barking insanity, the Deer's shootin' at em'. I got my rifle n' scope ready, put the barrel through the separations of the wood of the fence. Snuck it out there real good, I was completely hidden, this is the opportunity. Brock pulls Michael out the front door, n' the Deer comes out. I take the shot, near-blew his brains out if he hadn't moved, and it blast off half his right antler. It knocks that Deer back good, he's fallin' all over the ground, the kids are still screamin' in the livin' room. Brock runs in after the Deer, but the Deer panics, n' runs away. Just takes right off- he was gone. He was on the regain.

I hopped back over the fence right there and congratulated myself because I knew that I had utilized the environment to become it, n' then sniped em' up real good. But the Deer was still out there, he was still alive. As long as he's alive, y'all's gotta serious predicament.

I says to that family in there, "It ain't my fault that Deer came into your house, but I did shoot his girlfriend", n' left it at that. Walked right out that house out there, but I was skeptical. The Deer wasn't done with us. He's hoppin' round out there, plottin' to kill us.

Well we didn't know it, but Doug was runnin' after the Deer still, but the Deer was too fast, but Doug started firin' his gun n' shot that Deer right in the Butt Cheek! With a slap! The Deer turned around and started firin' his gun over n' over, his shots blank out, and Doug runs out too. And the Deer goes "Mhheeeeeerrrrrreeeeerrrrr!!" And Doug understood him. His Psychic Deer whisperin' abilities kicked in and he knew like a thang. He knew it like ya can't explain it, he knew, the Deer was sayin' "Let's Go Brandon."

Doug says, Why do you want to kill us? And the Deer goes "Mhhhherrrreeerr!" which means "You killed my girlfriend," in Deer language. Doug says, she shouldn't have been standing so close to the road where we could've seen her and wanted to shoot her. N' the Deer says "Mhhhereeerr!" n' Doug says "You kidnapped Betty Dollar! Now yer gonna die, Mother Bucker!"

Because, he was loadin' one he had in his pocket, puttin' it in the chamber, and right when he was ready to fire, the Deer shoots Doug with one last bullet he also had, put him down quick. The Deer ran off into the night. Doug was on the ground, still breathin' with the miracle of God in him. And,… we went home.

But it don't stop there… I went to the city the next day because I needed more ammo. My bullets was all over the highway, the last of what I had was wasted last night, I put about $2,000 dollars down on some bullets. Michael Taylor was bandaged up, Brock n' myself, we were all in the Store on a mission because we knew, at any moment, that Deer was gonna pop out of some bush and start firin' bullets at us. I took my gun in the store with my license to carry in hand, I was ready. I was real ready to kill that Deer. But we still didn't see it comin'.

Right through the city, the Deer was crawlin' through the Parkin' lot across the street from the Gun Store, layin' on the ground with the Scope Rifle pointed out from under the car. He was goin' fer the dirty shot, tryin'a get me back fer what I did to his antler that night. It stirred up inside em', n' made em' get all emotional, n' I was

just watchin' it. I don't know what's goin'
on, I'm just shootin' Deers. That's what I
do, I shoot Deers. Apparently the Deer went
to a Vet that night after Doug put a hole in
his ass. Gotta couple stitches on that ass,
that's right.

So I was in the Gun Store with Brock
n' Michael. We was talkin' to the Bald man
at the counter, had his sunglass on, I was
already buyin' the bullets, they were on the
glass counter. That's when the Bald man
said, "Keep yer eyes on the Parkin' lot, I
think there's a Sniper under the car over
there." We quickly ducked, as the store
window blew through like a sugar
explosion, and the Bald Man ran to the back
room. I got muh bullet, loaded the gun up, n'
peer round that corner, lookin' fer em'. I's
gonna get that son-um-itch, he's dancin' on
a thread with me. I caught a glimpse of him
under that red car right there, center of the
lot, I got my aim centered. I fired, Pow! Real
loud, shakin' the lot! The Deer ran off
through the parkin' lot. Didn't know where
he went, but that's just the first time that
day. He was scoutin' like a Chinese Spy. I
told Brock, we's needa get some clothes to
blend into the city environment if we's
gonna shoot this mother bucker.

I told him straight, "I've bout had it with this Deer, Imma put one right in his upper thigh, just to see the bullet wound get cooked on the BBQ. I'm a hungry man," I told him, "I'm hungry Brock. We're all hungry. We's gotta blend into the city environment."

Brock knew what to do. He took us all to the mall, took us into the Sports Section and we bought some Track pants and Track jackets for runnin' a long time, because in the city, everybody's runnin' round, doin' stuff. I got the stripes on my arms, and when I hold my rifle, it makes me feel like I'm wearin' Matrix Pajamas. We walked around inside the Mall because for once we thought that if the Deer tried to get in 'ere, that we'd have a clear vantage point to shoot the Deer, but the Security didn't like us because we's carryin' round buncha rifles n' shot guns n' everythin'. I said, don't you worry, we don't shoot people, we shoot animals. Just put em' up on the table, Brock can knock one out from about 100 yards- clean off- Poof like a powder puff.

Security wasn't too pleased, he says, "Y'all can get the hell out of the mall with yer guns or I'm callin' the Police." And that's when the Deer walked in…

This is what our suit looked like, we had some designer stuff on, with the stripes on the side, n' it was Track Suit stuff. But ya can't get my hat off muh head though, I'ma wear my hat, even if I'm wearin' Matrix Pajamas.

I seen that son-um-itch walkin' in all proud of em' dang self, had some aviators on with a Top Gun jacket on, thought he could fool us, but I knew better. I knew what I was gonna do right then and there, I pushed that security guy over cuz he was weak as hell anyway, and I got muh gun up, I was aimin' hard, ready to fire- I had a good shot in that moment too. I was gonna turn them light off that son-um-itch, get em' good. It was serious knockout waitin' on me, but the security guy got up n' grabbed my shoulders to stop me, and the shot got fired up in the air, the Deer spotted me, I got pissed. I punched that security guy in the face, I punched em' twice the son-um-itch, gettin' in-muh way like that. Knocked his dang lights out, I had to bend over to slap em' round so he don't die on meh. And in that moment, shot go fired o'er my head, knocked muh Carhart hat off.

The Boys got down and started pointin' their guns forward, a gun fight eruptit. Loud-as-hell, blastin' erewer. People screamin' ever-where, it was a dang rollercoaster, the Deer hada Shotgun. He popped a balloon. He fired at us chaotically. I aimed ahead, ready to shoot him but he was too close n' aimin' right at me- I ran.

I ran so fast. The Track suit got me equipped fer it, go it on me, started runnin', I's like a Flash. Now ya see meh, now ya don't. I was gone. I don't know where I went, I just found some long ass Hallway and went all the way down to the end. It had those yellowin' florescent lights n' everythin', it was kinda yellow. I could pee on the wall and nobody would know. But they knew I wouldn't do that cause this long ass hall leads to the restrooms. It's at the very end where yer biohazardous waste don't effect the oxygen of the rest of the shoppin' area. It's way back there.

But when I got to the back of the hall, I seen the sign on the door. It said OUT OF ORDER and the door was locked shut, I figure it ain't worth it. Probably looks like a dirt bike went through there. But when I turned round, there he was, lookin' at me from the other end of the Hall, holdin' that shotgun. He was gonna do it, I didn't hesitate, I pulled muh baby-maker out n' started peein' as hard I could, straight down the Hall, at least 40 yards- I punched myself in the stomache and WAM! Got that piss out past 50 with more water pressure. Hit em' right in the eye when he pulled the trigger, bust a hole in the wall. Gave me 'bout 30 seconds to run my fat ass down the Hall n' git the hell outta there. I ran at em'. Felt like full throttle up cliffside, just goin' fer it. Git right up to that Deer with muh Rifle and Pow! He punched me in the face. Got me good, got me real good, thought I cheated on somebody. He tried to come at me but his antlers wouldn't let him through the hall way without yankin' his head 'round, so he couldn't get no closer, I got the right Idea. I punched em' the dang face! Pegged that son-um-itch! Got em' good… got em' real good. I was aimin' fer the chest, but he took off runnin'. Now he's runnin' funny. Got that 'Sphincter tickle' walk, nailed that Son-um-itch n' made him squeal like a pig while playin' the banjo. I'm skilled, I know what I'm doin'. This is Inception.

Started runnin' on out after that Deer as my Boy's firin' in the background, he's a machine. He got gears. Deer dodges roun' a corner while he's loadin' it- I know he is, I seen it. He's gonna try n' shoot me.

I stopped runnin' at the Deer, and started runnin' away. Got back to Brock in the Taylors and I says we gotta git the hell outta here before it gets too serious. The whole Mall is cleared out, n' the police lights are out the window.

It's not what it looks like. I told the boys, the only way for us to walk outta here in one piece is with that Deer, so the Police will congratulate us for havin' our guns in the Mall, shootin' the dang thing. We agreed on it, n' we went back, further into the Mall, to find the Deer n' drag his ass out. There ain't no way out now. Not without a dead Deer anyway.

Brock and I started usin' Trashcans, started taking the square container that the trash can is in, and replacing it with skilled Deer hunters. We got mobilized across the Mall floor, lookin' to run up on that Deer. When we got to the other end of the mall, next to the food court and the vegetation ensemble with the trees n' stuff, we moved more cautiously. The Deer was hidin' somewhere. I knew he was in the vegetation thing, he couldn't be anywhere else. I pointed my gun at the tree through the trashcan hole n' fired a shot. Nothin'.

The Police swarm into the Food Court, there's at least a dozen of em'. They don't just walk in, or jog in, they strut in there, buncha cocky badges. You could tell one of em' was a little too happy, got that heated look on his face, me n' the boys shut up real tight, you could hear a butterfly fart in there. But then, suddenly I saw em'. He was over there… behind the counter. He was watchin' the whole thin' go on down right now. Seen the Police walkin' right in there. His Antlers were hidin' the whole time… wearin' a Chef hat in the kitchen, lookin' through the serve counter. He gotta long barrel pistol, most likely a 45 caliber, typa gun that's crafted especially *for* killin'. I don't know where they sell those in the Mall but somehow this Psycho Deer got one. It was like a Clown Pistol, you could pitch a small flag on it. It was shiny silver… got that real smooth shine to it. Dang near chrome 6 shooter with a manual hammer on the back, he wasn't buckin' round this time. He was calm, collectit. He was too relaxed, it was sociapathic. I looked over at Brock n' he was already gettin' his handgun out, he gotta basic Glock series- he seem em' too, he knows. Brock knew. He get's them 22s cuz we's go huntin', he like's to nail em' 3 er 4 times before they finally stop movin'. I didn't expect him to have a Glock at a time like this, but there it was, and there was no other way.

The Police er walkin' in there slowly with their gun drawn out, bein real cautious, they could feel the heat in the air. The deer's got its sights on em'. He was pointin' at the big one. I knew his game, I could see through em'. He was gonna take out the big one first, then pick the rest of em' off... one by one. Brock knew it too, but as long as no one fired their gun, the Police might go away... So Brock had his Glock pointed at the Deer, and the Deer had his gun pointed at the Big Police officer among the pack... there was too many of em'. I don't think the Deer wanted to shoot em' cause he knew if he did, they'd all start attackin' him.

So there we was, in the Mall food court, pointin' guns at the Deer while the Deer's pointin' his gun at the Police that have their guns drawn and ready murder. It's like... bein' camoed out, hidin' up in a tree when a Pack of wolves arrive. You just gotta ride it out. Just gotta wait for the Police to wander away, far away enough that you can get away yourself...

But then suddenly, Michael Taylor pulls a silencer barrel out of his pocket and handed it off to Brock with assassin like timin'. Brock screwed that one on real quick, that Glock already had a good push on it. N' this silencer, it was a special series Mike got from a Gun show in Dallas, and this Glock shoots like a Welrod gun usin' subsonic ammo, so that gun's only gonna give 'bout 74 decibel volume, bout as loud as slammin' a rickety ol' truck door.

Brock got that silencer on that gun quick, …real quick. He screwed it on there nice n' tight and pointed the barrel out at the Deer n' the Deer's still aimin' at the big one. But then one em' noticed him, he says, "Hey! That Deer's gotta Gun!"

The Deer shoots the big one- he drops onto the table like a sack of potatoes n' then a gun fight breaks out in the Mall food court at 3:59 pm. I could see the clock on the wall in my upper right peripheral. The Deer was behind the wall, the gun shots were outta control, they destroyed the cosmetic of the serve counter, that's a load of money right there, couldn't hold a flower without it wiltin'.

The insurance on a Police officer's gotta be a part of his check deductions, there's no other way. While the Police had their guns firin' at that sandwich serve counter, I seen that barrel again, pointin' round the corner of the 'Burrito Stand' Serve counter. This time, he was wearin' a sombrero over his antlers to hide em'. This Deer was good. If it wasn't for that long barrel… I wouldn't've noticed em'.

I signaled Brock to look at the Deer
at the Burrito stand, and Brock aimed his
Glock and silencer at the Deer's head. This
was it. This was the moment of truth, we's
abouta end it ferever n' go eat this son-um-
itch. Cut his leg off n' char it on the fire.

The Deer shoot's first, nails a couple
of em' and then they all started shootin' at
the Burrito Stand. Now, it's done. Ain't no
proper place to serve a Burrito in that
particular area right there. He went back to
the Sandwich one, still wearin' that
Sombrero, took a quick shot n' nailed
another police officer. Brock couldn't get a
good shot on em', I says, "Give it ta
Michael." But Brock didn't like that, he took
it real personal. Gave me that look like we
was gonna talk later.

I says, "Shoot that Psycho Deer bwoy!" Brock takes the shot. Shoots the sombrero right off the Deer's head- scares em' half to death, makes me more optimistic cause we's halfway there. Deer runs off into the back somewhere, so we pop out the trash thingys n' take chase. The Police are behind us yellin' freeze n' everythin' but they don't understand. We hop the counter n' start runnin' after the Deer through this long hall to the back door. The Deer runs out it and we're right behind em'. He's up there but we're gonna git his ass.

We chase em' out to an Alley inbetween the Mall, and the Deer takes cover behind a dumpster while we're shootin' like crazy. I could make a crazy 8 out of bullet holes on that dumpter- shot it so many times, tell ya what. The Police kept yellin' "It's the Russians! It's the Russians!" cause we're wearin' Track suits with the neon. I could smell em' comin' up the Hallway at us, they all got that 'P.O.'; 'Police Odor', y'all know what I'm talkin' bout'. It's like B.O. mixed with some Cologne or somethin', like a Rosey dog shit.

I slammed the door shut and moved the dumpster long ways up against the door, and then wedged another dumpster against

that one to double the weight right there.
Them dumpsters were packin'. Heavy-as-
hell. I turned up the heat real quick and
aimed my rifle at the Deer from behind the
dumpsters, aimin' out from the crack
between them, just like she said, an the shot
was fired. Hit a peanut butter jar between
the closed lid of the dumpster, right above
the Deers face, and that nutt butter splashed
out all over that Deer's eyes. Got it in the
eyes of em', he couldn't see a thang. He
started firin' erratically, I still got a shot left
in the gun. The doors maneuverin' the
dumpters, I try to shoot again, Pow!, but I
can't get a clean shot cause the Police are
wigglin' muh baracade. The Deer runs off,
smacks into a wall, and then runs the other
direction aimelessly- we run after em'. Deer
runs into a parked car, slam-sliding over the
hood like ice off the edge, tumblin' round,
staggerin' back up, running- SMACK into
this parked van.. slides up the side of the
side of the van, hits the tree, yanks his head
away from the tree as he's floppin' round on
the ground like a dang fish, he jumps, sprints
forward, Wap!, into a parked motorcycle,
flyin' over the handles, his hooves up in the
air like Batman the ride- just whoosh upside
down, lands on his back- he's sliding, his

head smacks into the bumper, he's spinnin',
his ass hits an ol' lady's shoppin cart, she's
adjustin' her glasses, the carts upside down.
The Deer kicks the Shoppin' cart, it hit's the
ol' lady's car and bounces groceries all over
her car, the Deer gets up quickly, his hooves
sliding the ground, like he was pealin' out
hard, 4 by 4 horses in Antarctica. And once
he caught traction, he was gone straight
down parking lot lane, cars backin' out the
way! They don't want that Deer ruinin' their
car, it was terrifyin', it was the most
outrageous thang I've seen.

The Deer turned around, started
firin' back at us n' then gets hit by a city
bus. We started runnin'… ya know… tried
to catch up with that son-um-itch, he's a
good 150 yards back there nah, that's a little
too far fer Brock's aim, but he's rebuildin'
his rifle right now 'cause he always cleans it
before his next kill. Bobby Dollar's a hungry
man, n' Brock Dollar's a good shot, but I
knew this wasn't the time, I told Brock, "We
needa hold off on the gun shots n' wait for
the Deer to tire himself out, wait for him to
be at his weakest point, then take em' out. 1,
2, 3." N' Brock knew. Michael Taylor was
runnin' far ahead of us though, and caught
up with the Deer finally gettin' up from that

bus accident, Michael punches the Deer in the face. They end up fightin' in the middle of the intersection, but it doesn't last long, the Deer kicks Michael's ass, knocked that poor judgement right the hell out. He just hit the ground, right there in the middle of the street and the Deer started Cryin' out like a monster, "Mhhheeeeeerrrrreeeeeerr!!!"

The Deer was already wearin' the Aviators, but then he took away Michael's Cigar n' put in his mouth, started puffin' on it. Blew that smoke right out like he was just the coolest dang deer ya ever did see. We all jumped to take cover behind the bus as the Deer started firin' the long barrel pistol at us. But that's when Doug pulled up in the Convertible cause muh Wife got pissed off about the pickup truck. The Police are drivin' up behind him. We all get into the Convertible, I grabbed Michael, n' threw him in the back seat, we went drivin' down the street after the Deer. He was runnin'. That convertible surprised us, I think it was the airbags, decent all-terrain vehicle in the urban environment. The ability to run over curbs and the shock absorption diminishes the accuracy interference so I can get a good clean shot. I nick named it 'Accomplice', cause all your vehicles gotta have a name, n' it's usually a woman's name.

The Deer was runnin' through the busy street with and against traffic dependin' on what side of the street he was hopin' to. We followed him on out down 2 major blocks before he cut left to a School Bus full of children, holds the driver up through the window n' forces him to stop. The Deer get onto the bus and kicks the school bus driver out of the bus! The Deer was drivin' now, the entire school bus was full of screamin' children.

I knew we had to do something because there was children on that bus. We had to get up close to that bus n' control the situation. Doug moved the car up to the side of the school bus and the Deer started firin' his gun at us through the windows, the little kids holdin' their ears tight. Brock jumped to a completely opened window and crawled into the school bus. The Deer saw em' n' got real frustrated with em'. The Deer left the driver seat and started fightin' Brock. The Bus is coasting in a straight line until the bus comes to a red light, passed through open section of the road but hits a dip in the road for the 2 gutters on either side of the intersection; the fighters are bouncing up in there, dang near sky surfin'.

The School bus veers off to the right, start roamin' out into an open park with tons-a-grass n trees n' everythin', that bus hit the curb n' drove right over the park. We drove the convertible over the curb after it, n' blew out the 2 back tires of the Bus with our great aim, which slowed it down good, *real* good. We catch up to the bus, I hop out the convertible n' walk up to the stopped Bus. The Deer punches Brock through the bus doors, he lands on his back, but it ain't nothin'. Brock shakes it off n' walks back to the bus n' swings at the Deer, punches him back good. Brock grabs that Deers leg n' yanked that Deer right outta that dang bus. The Deer got up quickly though, this Deer was a stubborn one, don't give a got-dang. He got back up in started fightin' Brock again, but Brock punched him again, knocked that Deer the hell out good. He was still breathin' but he was sleepin' hard. He's gettin' a Narcoleptic Sample.

The Police arrive, the kids defend us n' say we saved their lives n' all that, and the Deer was still alive so we was ready to kill it but ever-body got this "Protect the Wildlife" attitude, the Police tranquilized it.

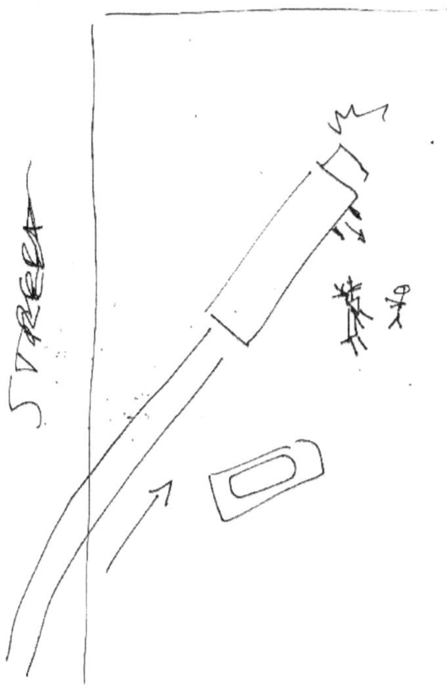

I kept tellin' em', "Y'all don't understand this Deer, he's gonna kill everbody one day. Ya'll are gonna die. Ya gotta kill em' now, while he can't react, while he's the most vulnerable, it's what Wild Predators do. They wait fer ya to be comfortable n' then.., when y'all completely distractit, they pounce ya. Eat ya alive, you're a Tummy friend after that.

I've seen all kinds of crazy thangs in my experience, I've seen it all, n' now, I know what a Psycho Deer is. I seen it here tonight, it was this Deer right here. He snapped. He ate too many psychedelic lichens off the stone edges. Ya gotta shoot him now, before it's too late."

Course, no one wanted to hear that n' started criticizin' us fer bein' animal murderers that don't feel nothin' fer no one, like it's a bad thing. I mean the part where I don't feel nothin' fer no one, that's a neutral thing. This is America. I'm an Animal Predator. I Hunt Deers. Talkin' bout us like we're Psychopaths er somethin', I told em' all ta shut up. Told em' right there, everbody shut yer dang mouth right now n' listen to me, I said it fer real, I says, "This ain't no Rudoplh the Red Nose Reindeer, he ain't sniffin' snow in Alaska. This a Psycho Deer, it's dangerous, it's got a plan to kill er'body, at any moment."

They weren't buyin' it, I got pissed, I said "y'all dumb pricks are gonna die if y'all don't kill this Deer right now." This Environmentalist in the crowd around the situation in the park says, "He's just a scared animal." I says, "You mother-… you have no idea what y'all talkin' bout.

Y'all are out of line." And he says, "You're out of line, you're an Animal Murderer," n' ever-thin'. I said, "I shoot an Illegal Aliens smugglin' Drugs across the boarder n' you're okay with it, but when I shoot a Deer's ass for dinner, yer balls get sucked right back up into yer asshole. Yer makin' me ask question, like how is that humanly possible?" Everyone got pissed off at me, and the Police forced me n' the boys to leave. We got in our Convertible and drove around the corner, but we knew it wasn't over yet. Michael's still passed out in the back seat with Doug. Brock's passenger side. I park the convertible near the street curb close to the corner so we could spy on the situation from across the park. We're both lookin' through binoculars, we were watchin' the whole thing go down from far away. Binoculars lookin' out the winda at the calm befer the storm. They already moved the kids out, so they're gone. The Tow truck showed up, n' then there was these environmentalist Veterinarians assistin' the Deer. Of course, it wakes up n' you can hear screamin' in the distance. Brocks grabbin' his rifle, I says wait boy,… let em' learn their lesson first. …

…okay now get ready… and he started aimin' his rifle out over the rear side mirror, gettin' that precision aim on a solid restin' point. Brock says, "We're too far away, he's too small in the scope." I told him not to worry, my Maven RS.1 I got from Wyoming is made of Japanese glass with 15 times the Zoom; the most accurate scope you can put on a rifle. 14 Inches.

Brock got it on his gun, started lookin' through it, the police are in a gun war with the Deer. It's outright Deer Terrorism. I seen it through muh own binoculars. They didn't wanna trust the experts, the people with the Deer experience, they'd rather try n' psychologically manipulate the Deer. That thing woke up n' lost it's mind. Brock says, "This is better, But he's movin' around too much, I don't have a clean shot."

I said, put the gun down, and we went for a little ride back, to get closer to the scene of the Deer. I drove right over the curb through the bushes into the area and honked the horn, made sure the Deer could see us comin. I stop the car. The Deer's off in the distance, I said to Brock, "Put his lights out boy." N' Pow! Nails the Gun right out of the Deer's hooves!

I don't know how he hold's em', I just seen him with these guns, pullin' the trigger. Deer gets mad, starts runnin' away again. Brock fires the gun again, and hits the wall just right of the Deer as it's runnin' away. I didn't even keep goin. I told em', "boys, I'm hungry. Alright? I been dealin' with this dang Deer all day long, I needa touch back, get my head in the game. I asked Doug, "Where is the nearest Steak House?" N' that's where we headed. But Brock says, "When we get there, we gotta be ready. The Deer could strike at any moment, he's determined. He's lookin' for a moment to strike. And I agreed with em', we'll be ready. It won't be long before the Deer finds us. But if the Sun was goin' down, I was gonna need my night vision goggles so I can see him before he sees us.

The sunset was orange n' then purple, and then night fell. We was at the steak house in our Track suits. Michael's finally awake and looks like a Deer beat the hell out of him. You couldn't fix his hair with concrete. Brocks got some black eyes and bubbled up swollen lip. His eyebrows swollen. There's blood all over his mouth. He was tore up. Doug was bandaged on his arm and over his nose. I was just fine.

We sat at the dining table in the
Steakhouse. The waiter came to the table,
we all ordered Rib Eyes and Beer and we ate
up, had a good time. But we didn't know…
just out the window, across the street,
behind some car over there, The Deer was
hidin' with a gun.

We had good ribeye that night. Some
of the best ribeye I've ever had. It was juicy,
fattening, and it made your soul roar like a
lion. It came with potatoes n' Bacon n'
butter on the side, salt n' pepper, sour
cream. I shake the salt n' pepper over the top
3 times first, Then,… I put the Sour cream…
on the potatoes, after I put the butter on top.
I stir it together with my fork, impale that
potatoe, and eat it with that greesy Bacon
kabobbed on the fork. Just puts a hole in
your lip ever-time ya eat it.

Got us all some high content Dark
Lagers and we drank em'. It took the edge
off. I was fulfilled inside me. Then I paid for
the meal, the Waiter came up to us, took the
card, he brought it back, I left a $40 tip,
signed off the receipt, we got up, we was
about to leave. But then Doug says, "I gotta
use the restroom," and then everyone had to
so, we were still there, only we were
thanking them in a different way.

We were expressin' our thanks. But
as soon as we stepped out, someone pointed
out the window n' said, "Hey, that Deer's
gotta gun!"

We got down quickly as the shot
fired through the window, nearly blew muh
head clean off. Everyone got down,
screamin' bloody murder, I was sick of it.
Michael lit up another cigar right there in the
restaurant cause the ice was already broken.
I told the boys, "Look, he's just gonna keep
doin' this and I need a break right now. So I
say we head on home and deal with the Deer
later." And that's what we did. The Deer
was shootin' the windows out, and then we
ran to the Convertible and tore ass down the
street. The Deer couldn't catch us. I figured
I *could* take a break from this Psycho Deer
fer now but he'd be back. Ya just gotta
accept the fact that the Deer is out there n'
he won't quit.

So, in the car ride back home I
started given er'one the Poop-show cause
we couldn't shoot a deer with in 10 ft, yet
we could hunt down a fresh doe grazin' a
drink on the lake side at 50 meters. I says to
Michael, "yer kids in the hospital cause of
this Deer n' you let em' beat yer ass, you
should be ashamed of yer self."

But Michael didn't care, he just stared out at the passin' view, puffin' that dang cigar like he's plottin' a Conspiracy. Told Doug, all he's good for is a "psychic hotline", n' told my son I was disappointed in his aim- "the Deer was right there in the service winda." Brock defended himself- says the sombrero looked like a crooked target- I says "the next time y'all see a face next to a target, y'all shoot the face first. Let this be a lesson to ya boy. Ain't no one gonna put their face next to a target unless they wanna get shot in the face." I made an example for him, "think about the time y'all went to the circus, n' they have that squirt gun thingy with the people Putin' their face in the hole n' ya gotta shoot 'em in the face with the squirt gun, only they put their face next to a target n' y'all just go right ahead n' Spray that face clean off the neck. No harm, no foul."

Doug got angry n' says he's an archer. "I been trained muh whole life to shoot bow n' arrow! Now when it's most important, all y'all gots is guns! It ain't my fault y'all don't got big ass arms like me" n' ever-than'– n' he ain't lyin'. He could arm wrestle a dang grizzly bear.

I told em' "you're right Doug, I sincerely apologize from the bottom 'my heart, didn't mean to put you down like that, …I meant to put ever-one else down though. We can be better, I know it. It's that Pep-talk psychology right there.

We got back to the Cabin, n' life went back to normal fer 'bout 12 hours. It's about 8 PM, The Taylor's went back home n' Brock went to sleep up in his bedroom. At 6 in the mornin', I was on the couch cleanin' my gun that I took apart. I could get it back together in 60 seconds. My wife went to pour me a glass of Orange Juice sittin' on the counter with mornin' sun comin' through the winda, when a bullet burst through the glass n' exploded that glass of Orange Juice all over the kitchen. My wife screamed.

I yelled, "Don't waste your breath, Betty! It's just that dumb Deer out there… thinks he can work a gun. I didn't realize how ridiculous it was until we was chasin em' across the City Mall. Dumbass Deer got eyes on either side of his head, wouldn't know what straight was if he was gay in the NRA- That dumbass Deer couldn't hit an Antarctic blue whale in a German Dirigible; fires a gun like that cross-eyed weasel.

"But I digress… a stupid bullet *IS also* a wild bullet. It's still dangerous."

Another bullet swooped in, blew my breakfast right off the counter- split the plate in 2- my toast was still there though. That got me real angry, and Betty wasn't too obliged. Says to me, "Bobby Dollar, y'all better shoot that Deer to death er' the love-time maintenance is compromised, that'll be it, I have spoken." When Betty means business, Betty means business. That was the moment I knew I had to face the music, go on out there n' stop that Deer once n' fer all. He's gone from Psycho to a Serial Cock-blocker. Y'all can put a psycho in a padded room but a Cock-blocker don't deserve four seasons. That typa shenanigans deserves 6 months solitary confinement n' a kick in the nuts every Sunday at 7 AM.

I pointed my gun out the door and shot my Magnum- had a real kick on it, blew me back against the wall, my hat flew off, but the Deer ran away. I knew this was gonna have to be settled on our land, in the mountains, usin' our camo gear in ready-to-go position so that we are ready to go at any moment. The Jeep got replaced by my insurance and was dropped off outside the Cabin on delivery.

Same model, different color. This one's got mountain Camo. The whole thang, just looks like sticks n' dirt and trees. I took Brock in it fer a ride into town which is just down the road about a half mile from the Cabin. The Taylors were at the Bar next to the Gas Station of the main strip. The Grocery store's across the street, there's some Antique shops, a Mexican Restaurant, a Salon, and a small hardware slash gun store next to the Bank in a culdesac. It's like the basics round them parts, nothin' too much. I get muh donuts at the Bar, they serve coffee too but I don't drink coffee unless I feel like it.

Parked the Jeep right there at the Bar, n' we walked into the Bar, Brock sat at the Bar, n' I stood at it when the Taylors walk in and sit next to us sayin' we gotta talk n' ever-thin'. The Bartender came out, and he caught me off guard because he had this really big black afro. I didn't want to be disrespectful, so I looked away real quick cause it was really stupid. I don't wanna give em' the impression that his afro is stupid even though it's *really* stupid. The Bar tender was cleanin' a glass, towels over each hand, one holdin' the glass, the other pushing the towel into the glass.

I didn't wanna look up cause I knew if I did… I was gonna laugh… I was gonna lose my grip n' this poor man's gonna have to face the embarrassment… I don't wanna do that to him because I'm respectful, but Brock says, "Have I seen you before?"

The Bartender says, "Meh."

I gave Brock the Stink eye, told him to have some respect. But Brock was determined, he says, "Naw, I think I seen ya before."

The Bartender says, "Meh."

Michael's not payin' attention, he puts his hand on the counter n' says, dark lagers, all 'round.

The Bartender says, "Meh." Clops over to the other side of the bar n' starts pourin' us the beers. I says to Michael, we gotta find this Deer, where ever it is, n' we gotta kill it. It's affectin' muh marriage now, it's gotta stop. It was one thing to drive my wife's truck that night but… now she's awake when the Deer strikes. That' changes ever-thin'.

The Bartender clops over to us and sets the plate of Beers down on the counter, n' we all grab one, or I passed on to Brock, whatever.

Michael says, "I know of a Cemetery where the scary stuff is. Weird Ghosts er' roamin' roun' out there." He was basically sayin' we should lure the Deer out to the Cemetery n' kill it there so that the ghost of the Deer would be stuck in the Cemetery, but I objected.

I says, "What if I got a relative in there that I like to visit n' I can't cause the Deer Ghost is shootin' Ghost Bullets past my head all the time? I want peace n' quiet when I'm in a Cemetery." And we all agreed, the Deer *shouldn't* die in the Cemetery. But then that begged the real question right there, where do we wanna kill this son-um-itch? Doug says, "I wanna kill him at a gun range." Brock says, "No. We gotta kill em' in the wild, so that he becomes one with the forest, and the evil can be devoured by the spirit of the Earth."

I says, "I don't care where he dies, as long as he ain't alive." Took a drink-a-muh-beer, put it half down, dropped the bottle on the counter in told em', "Where the hell is he? That's what I wanna know."

The Bartender says, "Meh." As he clops over to us and sets another plate of beers down for us. Everyone finished quickly cause I was already done and they needed to keep up. We were on our next beer. Brock says, "I think the Deer is schemin' back at that creepy old house in the woods that we found with Boomer last night."

I ask em', "Why do ya think he does it?" n' Michael started ramblin' on about how it's the ghost of the haunted house possessin' the Deer… talk bout it bein' an unrested Deer ghost that I shot in the past. It lingered in that house n' possessed a livin' Deer n' now that Deer ghost is inside the livin' Deer somewhere. It's not the same as Pet Cemetery. I don't even know if that's true. All I know is that Deer is out there, and it's motivated to a killin'.

Bartender serves up another plate of Beer, we're double fistin' these bottles, the Bartender was very kind. I made the comment that we should tip him now, show our appreciation, but our hands were full.

The Bartender says, "Meh."

N' then, that's when the Old Man with the Wizard hat started talkin' to us.

He says, Yea, "I think I know about this Deer you're looking for."

I says, Yeah? N' he says. "Yes. I'm absolutely certain."

N' I's like, "Spit it out bwoy! What do y'all know bout this dang Deer?!"

He says, "I seen the Deer in this very Bar…"

Brock was irritated, says, "We're talkin' a real live Deer."

Old Man says, "I seen it. Walkin' on it's hind legs… walkin' through the woods in the middle of the night, creepin' the dang Bears out. For some Bears It's the opportune time to hunt- in the middle of the night, catch it while it's sleepin'! Bears r' sneeky ruthless predators. Then here comes this Deer, walkin' on it's hind legs, holdin' a shot gun at 3 AM in the deadest part of the woods, you know somethin' ain't right. You gotta put it down. When you see that Deer, you put it down, son. You put it down. N' once it's done… Y'all pray it never happens again. Amen."

N' he was serious bout it. You could see it in his eyes, he meant ever-word. I got ta thinkin' it might be a good time to search this Bar for the Deer, n' I drew my gun. Said to the boys, "That Deer's in here." Bartender came up and served another plate of beers. I downed the 2nd one, then grabbed the 4th one, I told the Bartender, "You are an awesome bartender. It's the *way* that you provide, that *is* the great work." Then Michael looked up at the Bartender n' says, "Hey, Wait a minute! You're not the Bartender! You're that Dang Deer!"

The Bartender says, "Mhhheeerrrr!"

Everyone pulls out there guns n' jumps for cover as gun shots fly ever-where! Tables tipped over, the Deer's behind the counter, the Old Man just walks right up to the counter as we're shootin' back n' forth, n' the Oldman just POW!

Nail's the Deer in the head.

Kills him!

That was it.

It was over.

Put the Deer's lights out.

The Old Man shot him before we did. Or so he thinks, because I think it's negotiable, I'm pretty sure it was my shot that hit the Deer in the head. N' so he started fightin' me on it, n' I said, "No, I'm pretty sure that was my bullet shot that put the Deer's lights out so, I'm the one that get's to take the kill home.

Old Man got pissed, says he shot that Deer fair n' square. Says *HE'S* takin' the corpse home and that *HE* shot the Deer.

I says to em' with my handgun by muh leg, says, "I don't think y'all understand mister. That Deer is my Deer. It's been chasin' my ass fer a hot minute. I'm bout to take em' home n' eat em." I was so drunk, n' ever-one else was drunk, n' that Old Man was bein' such a prick that I pointed my finger in his face real sternly, n' the other boys click checked their guns. Dollar Nation. Step aside. Brock grabbed the Deer by the Antlers n dragged the Deer over the top of the bar like a thick bundle of blankets, just… floppin' on the floor. He's a strong boy. He knows how to pick it off, n' then take it home.

The Old Man says "Stop! I'm callin' my Attorney!"

So, I guess he got that Attorney on the phone, they got to talkin', I told em' all to shut up, is what I did. We took that Deer out the door, put it in the Jeep, they came outside sayin' stuff and I just says "Shut the Hell Up. It's mine!"

The Attorney says she's gonna sue us, n' I said, "Fer what?" n' she says "fer stealin' newly obtained property by the evidence of the legal owner."

I got frustrated cuz I don't wanna put up with anymore Government stuff, n' I told that Attorney, "You're defendin' a guy that didn't rightfully obtain this property. It's my Deer! I shot em'! I'll put em' on a rocket into space with an electric car if I want to! Stop me!" We strapped that Deer onto the Jeep, n' we take off with that Deer.

Halfway down the road, the Deer comes back to life! The Jeep rocks back n' forth. I pull over, the Deer breaks free, it runs off into the forest. Perfect timin' the Police arrive as the Deer's gone, and the Old Man drive up in his VW bug, get's out, starts screamin' about how we're the ones who stole the Deer. I pointed to the roof of my Jeep n' says, "Wouldn't that be convenient if it were true? I'd cut you a leg off right now just to bribe ya to go away."

So either way, the Deer was gone, the Old Man didn't have anything on us, and the Deer was actually gone. The Old Man started accusin' us of putting the Deer in Earth orbit with an electric car, n' I knew we was off the hook. I was goin' home soon. Get back to the drawin' board on this Deer, n' that's exactly what happened. Officer sent us home, n' home we went, but then…

Then I started to really think bout it. This was weird, he was too weird. Creepy weird. Indeerin'. Like Inhuman but more like Indeerin', but in a negative perspective. I didn't even go in the Cabin, I was outside, pacin' the driveway. My eyes got real big as I was pacin' the driveway, like I's lookin' at the ground in deep contemplation, waitin' fer that Deer. Thinkin' he might interrupt my pace at any moment n' I'd blow it's dang head off. Michael came back to me in his 4x4 Truck n' says they found the Deer up the road, n' the Old Man got it back. It's dead. It must've had some kind of last psychotic twitch before it died completely.

I didn't believe him, I says, "Michael you know it ain't true. You know this Deer is different."

Michael says, "I seen it." n' it got all mellow dramatic n' ever-thin'. I says "That Deer is demonic or somethin', it got right back up n' jumped off the truck. I don't think that Old Man shot him. That Deer gotta gun, Mike. He's weildin' a 6 shooter while walkin' round on his hind legs. It's a monster. It's somethin' Evil. I gotta see this Deer fer myself, I gotta know he's dead."

Michael says "We're not allowed to see the Deer because it's on a bigger level." N' I respect that. But that also makes me suspicious that the Deer may have faked his death. I think he shot another Deer in the Wild, brought that Deer back to the site where he jumped off the Jeep, n' now that Deer is the Old Man's Dinner, n' the Psycho Deer is still out there.

Doug started sayin' it's cause of the Psychedelic Lichens. He says they eat it and trip like they're higher than space. I figure if that Deer was high on Psychedelic Lichens when he was attackin' us in the beginnin' that the Deer maybe comin' down from it er somethin'… maybe he's got a messed up hangover but he's still out there, I know he is. The Psycho Deer was too good. He's differnt. Really, in the end, if it really is those Psychedelic Lichens, I gotta look inta that.

So days went by. My wife unsuspended the maintenance n' no gun shot's were fired, it was a decent week, but it would've been better if gunshots *were* fired. But I was constantly lookin' round, suspectin' that at any moment that this Deer was gonna shoot me without suspectin' it. It was in the back of my mind the whole time, and I knew that the moment he tried- I was already more than ready, I had an entire agile scheme strategy, I was ready ta corner his ass n' cut off his head. Huntin's what I do.

A Month went by n' it was quiet. Michael came by to visit n' says a buncha stuff bout the business. I told em' I was gonna go huntin' this afternoon.

He brought up the Psycho Deer n' I says he's out there. He goes "The Deer died, Bobby Dollar." He goes, "That Deer died in the forest after he jumped off the Jeep." I told him I didn't believe that.

I says, "The Deer's waitin' out there to pop a skull the same way a 65 Cal pops a Water balloon. I don't believe fer a nothin' that Deer is dead. He's-a-waitin'. He's out there waitin' to kill me at just the right time."

Michael started lookin' at me like I needed a Vacation. Says, "Bobby, you needa get out. You needa get a grip. This Psycho Deer stuff is over. Ya gotta let it go."

But I knew he was the one that was lettin' go too soon. It was too soon. I knew the Deer was out there. But Michael insisted, "Look," he says, "I know of a Bowlin' Alley at the Edge of Town before it cuts off inta the City. It's got a lot of people, a lot of fresh air, plenty of beer, the Heroin junkies in the back are playin' Dice for Dollars, it's a great place.

I said Okay.

So we went to the Bowlin' Alley n' it was still surrounded by the forest. The place looked like a Log Cabin Lodge. It was big but made to look like real tree logs… maybe fer decoration. Got inside there, gained access, wiggled around a bit, n' we was playin' ball. As soon as I walked in, I could feel em' watchin' me. I could feel the Psycho Deer's eyes, pearin' out at me.

He was there somewhere, I knew it… So anyway, I was rollin' strikes all night cause of muh technique. Sometimes I do the Ball Scratcher. Get er' down the lane n' hit the sweet spot. Pow! That Lane will ride yer 2 fingers all night if ya know how to treat it right. We were havin' a great time. When suddenly my Beer glass exploded, sittin' on the table next to the Bowlin' Ball Retractin' thing-a-ma-jiggo. It just blew up, n' I knew it was him. No one heard the bullet shot cause-a-the way it happened but I knew it was a Silencer, at least below 80 decibels. No one thought anythin' of it n' played like nothin' happened. Some-kinda-pop in the electricity er' something. Even Michael looked at the glass and says, "Don't worry, the ice probably broke the glass."

I says "No ya stupid man, this a Psycho Deer attempt! He aims like an ass hole."

Michael says if I pull muh guns out n' start shootin' we's can't get away cause we're still wearin' the bowlin' shoes n' then the Police will have their real shoes n' use some C.S.I. stuff on the soul of the shoe that would lead them back to my Cabin in the woods. N' I says "Well I'm gettin' the Hell out of here."

So I went to the Desk to get muh shoes back. …I couldn't handle it. The Service lady puts her soda pop glass on the counter and it explodes. I freak out- pull my gun out, point it around! She laugh at me, says, "Oh that's just these weak ass glasses, they can't handle cold temperature.

I was so pissed off. I went home pissed off. When I got home, I was pissed off. I was pissed off when I opened the front door, n' then pissed off when I shut it behind me. Pissed off at the Dinner Table. Pissed off on the shitter. Pissed off watchin' TV. I was pissed off. The Deer's out there sittin' pretty, n' all this stuff starts happenin' that's makin' me look stupid. I'm pissed!

A few months go by, n' I'm still paranoid bout it. Wife says, "Maybe it's time ya'll talk to somebody bout it, like a therapist er' somethin'." I says no way, they mind screw ya, I don't need no therapy. I'm fine. But she was serious. N' then I got pissed off. I got real pissed off. I stepped up from the table n' started stompin' up n' down the hall way. I says "There's a Deer out there that faked it's Death, Betty! He could strike at any moment!"

She yells at me, "Look at you Bobby! Look what these guns did to you!"

I yelled back, "Guns didn't do this! A Deer did! I can't believe you would think the Deer is dead after ever-thin' that's happened!"

She goes, "You gotta let it go, Bobby Dollar, he's a dead Deer now. It's over. It's in the past." I yanked my arm away from her hand, I couldn't admit to myself that she was that naïve. It was too late though, I already did. N' then she goes on, "All this Deer ever caused you is Pain and Fear Bobby" swear I was in a Soapy Series, "Bobby, think about the good things in life like Beer, n' Shootin' guns, n' eatin' dead Deers."

I told er, "I can't think about none those thangs without that Psycho Deer in it." Then I looked away and says to er' "It's spiritual, he's still alive, sharpenin' his knife in the forest… in that creepy ass house.

She asks me, "What creepy old house? You mean the one far back behind our Property?"

"Yea, that one."

She says, "That's where I go to cry."

I says, "What the hell you talkin' 'bout Betty, there's plenty of better places to cry. You could cry in the bathroom, the kitchen… You can use the garage if ya want…" but she insisted, that she goes out there on summer days and pins pictures up in the house to remember our Cabin days. I told her she's Bipolar n' that she needs to see a therapist to talk about the good things in life n lettin' go of somethin'.

I says, "One day that Deer is gonna try to shoot me down Betty, but I'm gonna come out on top, you wait n' see, I'm always on top." N' she agreed that I *am* always on top. No doubt. It was a good omen. A foreshadow. Destiney waitin' ta pass. It was written in the tea leaves of the Steak seasonin'. I'm a time bomb.

Nearly a Year goes by n' nothin's happened, I didn't even think bout it that much, when suddenly I get a piece of fancy paper mail with a letter inside address to 'The Four Huntsmen'. It invited us to go to a special dinner with free food n' free booze, a function that's celebrating Good Deer Hunters. My red-flad-ometer popped up n' I considered, this could be the Psycho Deer, but nothing had come of the Psycho Deer for so long that I doubted it.

I talked to Brock about the Invitation n' he asked if he had to dress presentable, I

says "It would be much appreciated."
Talked to Michael, Doug n' Tommy bout it
n' they says they're goin' just cause they
"were the reason a Good Deer Hunter gets
congratulated." Cocky brats, gotta love em'.

So the day arrives. Betty comes with
me. The whole Hunter Family arrives at this
Fancy Dinner Restaurant in the City along
with several other Hunters of the mountains.
We're all seated, there's 6 of us. The 3
Taylors; Michael, Doug, Tommy, and the 3
Dollars; Bobby, Betty, and Brock. We got a
big table. We was lookin' through the Menu.
They brought us all Dark Lagers without
askin' for em'. The Beer was good. I started
lookin' round n' noticed there was a
Balcony that overlooked the restaurant. N'
when I saw who was in that blacony, it was
a Deer with an eyepatch, a mustache,
wearin' a black cowboy hat on his antlers,
smoking a cigar. That's when the Brazilian
in a white tuxedo walked up n' started sayin'
stuff like "This message is from the Psycho
Deer. He's watchin' y'all right now. But
little did you know, there's a bomb under
the floor of the table that can blow up a 30
feet radius in 20 seconds. The Psycho Deer
says, if you walk away from this restaurant,
y'all explode. But, if y'all drink all the beer

in the restaurant, you can leave n' we'll never cross paths again."

The Brazilian man walks away and we start chuggin' the beer. With Brock around, I wasn't sure we could get em' piss drunk so it was already fun. I think Brock crushed 22 beers n' that sit before he fell over unconscious. Put some aspirin in his chest pocket. The Restaurant ran out of beers to serve us, n' we all stood up from the table cause we all needed a piss. The boys headed straight back to the restroom n' I followed behind. We got to the stairway that leads up to the balcony, took it out n' started pissin' up the staircase as I came in through the door up there, pissed all over the dinner plates on the tables, ever-one was astounded, n' then there was that dang Psycho Deer! I pull out my gun, n' POW! Shot that Deer while I was pissin' on that Deer! First ever Lethal Piss Shot in Huntin' History. The People are scared outta their minds, they're runnin out the balcony. The boys head up into the balcony, they pull out their guns n' they unload on that Deer Corpse. If it wasn't dead before, it's an inanimate object now. Coulda burned a leopard print on that ass, shot it so many times. Michael ashed his Cigar out on the Deer. Brock spit on the

Deer. But then, the Deer dropped the button he was holdin' and the table in the Restaurant exploded. Ever-one was gone already anyway, n' the police were on their way, we had to get this Deer Carcass outta here.

The 5 of us Dragged the Deer out to the convertible, we put the Deer in the back seat, bleedin' out all over the dang car. N' I don't remember what else happened, but I got in and started drivin home with Betty in the seat next to me, n' Brock in the back with the Deer corpse. Next thang you know, I got lights beeming into muh mirrors, flashin' ever-where, I told Betty, "don't let the aliens near my ass Betty." But it was the Police again. N' then that's where we're at right now. So basically, I wasn't plannin' on bein' this drunk, I was forced to be drunk by the dead Deer in the back of the convertible that was stolen by that exact same Deer a year earlier when it was tryin'a kill me. N' I was drivin' drunk in the convertible because no one was sober enough to drive so I had to take responsibility fer muh family, that's why we're in Jail right now, so that I can finally live with myself. It's all because of that Psycho Deer. N' I'm glad he's dead, because now I can sleep peacefully.

N' if another Psycho Deer ever exists, just gimme a call, I'll kill the shit outta *that* Deer too. I don't deserve no D.U.I. because my name's Bobby Dollar, n' I'm a Hero n' a Patriot! God Bless America! God Bless the United States! God Bless the United States Constitution, and I hope who ever disrespects it gets killed fer treason! Let's go Brandon!

POLICE REPORT

Bobby Dollar was found intoxicated, carrying a firearm while driving behind the wheel of a stolen white Convertible Car with his wife, Son, and what appeared to be a dead Deer corpse at 6pm on Saturday afternoon. The car originally belonged to a visiting cousin of the Barrymore's at a Cabin not far from Bobby Dollar's Cabin. The Man inside the Deer was Colin Flint. He's a costume mastermind and psychopath that teaches occult practices. He'd had an affair with Betty inside the Creepy old house with the pictures in it. Colin premeditated to kill the family and start a new one with Betty Dollar. However, Colin went to the hospital the last time he had to run from the Four Huntsman. He tried to take a hiatus n' got a job working at a Bar as a Deer, only to run into the Four Huntsmen again and nearly died. Yes, that's right… the Psycho Deer wasn't actually a Deer at all… it was just some dickhead impersonating a Deer that wanted to continue an affair with Betty Dollar, found shot to death inside a Bio-Mechanical Deer. Doug is not Psychic.

Books by Daniel Jacobs Nÿkkýnn

Chroska (2023)

Considerations (2021)

Cataclysma (2020)

MSPA (2015)

Vein Cupid (2015)

My Current Opinion (2013)

America 51 (2012)

Fatalgeist (2012)

For more information about any
of the above titles, visit:
nykkynn.com

"If it's Obvious, then it's true."
- *Daniel Jacobs Nykkynn*
Award Winning Battle DJ, Groundbreaking
Music Scientist, Author of multiple books…
Filmmaker, Game Maker, and overall
acclaimed 'Creative Mastermind'…

www.ingramcontent.com/pod-product-compliance
Lightning Source LLC
Chambersburg PA
CBHW020605160726
47991CB00002B/881